Other books in the Macy's World series:

Hair, It's a Family Affair

First published in 2021 by Cassava Republic Press

©Text and illustration: Mylo Freeman

ISBN: 978-1-913175-18-4

A CIP catalogue record for this book is available from the British Library.

Printed and bound in Europe by Akcent Media.

www.cassavarepublic.biz
www.mylofreeman.com

Macy's W♥rld

Smile
with
African Style

MYLO FREEMAN

CASSAVA | REPUBLIC

"Good morning Miss Brown, you look lovely today!"
says Macy. In a chorus, the children shout out,
"Yes, your dress is pretty, Miss Brown."

"Thank you, class! If you look closely, you'll notice it's a typical print fabric from **West Africa**," Miss Brown says.

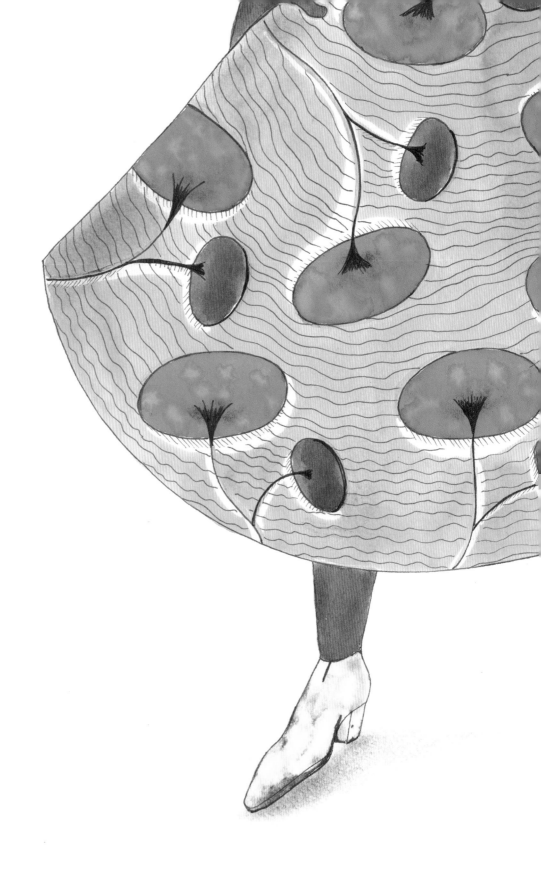

"Miss Brown, I have an idea, can we all come to school
next week wearing an outfit from different African countries?"
Macy asks.
"What a fabulous idea, Macy!"

The following week, Naomi is the first to arrive.
"I can see your dress is from Kenya,"
says Miss Brown.

"Yes, I am dressed as a Masai girl!" Naomi smiles.

EGYPT

SUDAN

SOMALIA

ETHIOPIA

RICAN
lic

UGANDA

KENYA

RWANDA
BURUNDI

TIC REPUBLIC
CONGO

TANZANIA

ZAMBIA

MALAWI

ZIMBABWE

MOZAMBIQUE

MADAGASCAR

BOTSWANA

SOUTH
AFRICA

"Good morning Naomi," says Sam.
"Look, my Kente robe is from the **Ashanti** people
in **Ghana** and Troy's outfit is from **Angola**!"

"Good morning Mimi. I love all those colorful beads, where is your dress from?" Miss Brown asks.

"From Ethiopia!" Mimi answers proudly.

Meanwhile Nahla has entered the classroom. "I'm dressed as a **Herero** lady from **Namibia**," she calls out cheerfully.

"And how do you like my Agbada from Nigeria?"
Mosope asks.

Everyone agrees that Mosope looks really cool.

"I'm a **Tutsi** warrior from **Rwanda**!" Femi calls out.

"And my clothes are from South Africa," says
Malika. "Ndebele people love a riot of colors."

But who is that and where is he from?

"My outfit is from Cameroon!" the elephant mask replies.

All the children have arrived except for Macy. "It's already late, where can she be?" Miss Brown wonders.

There she is!

"Look Miss Brown, you and I are wearing the same **necklaces**."

Macy laughs. "Both our outfits are **Igbo** style from **Nigeria**!"

More from Mylo Freeman,
author of the *Princess Arabella* series:

Hair, It's a Family Affair!

A celebration of black hair, through the vibrant and varied hairstyles found in a single family. With Mylo Freeman's trademark colorful illustrations, this entertaining book will show young black children the joys that can be found through their hair, and remind other children of the many different types of hair that can be found in the world around them.

ISBN: 978-1911115687

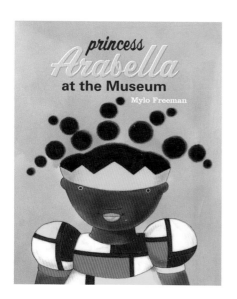

Princess Arabella at the Museum

Princess Arabella and her friends go to the museum. There are works of different artists exhibited: some are big and others are small. In some works you can lose yourself and others make you smile. Then the children want to go home. Why? Because they want to make their own work of art!

ISBN: 978-1913175061

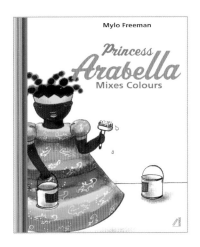

Princess Arabella Mixes Colors

Princess Arabella thinks her room is boring. So she decides she's going to do something about that – all by herself. She mixes up some paint and in no time at all her room looks fabulous.

A delightful picture book with fun information about mixing colors.

ISBN: 978-1911115366

Princess Arabella Goes to School

Princess Arabella and her friends embark upon their first day at Princess School. They find themselves taking some very unusual lessons – and when they are allowed to bring their pets to school, fun and games ensue!

ISBN: 978-1911115656

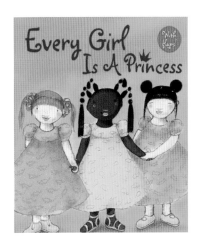

Every Girl is a Princess

In this book, you'll meet princesses from all over the world. They all have their favourite animal and their own crown. But who fits the remaining crown?

A cheerful and colorful picture book that shows that a little princess (or prince) hides in every child.

ISBN: 978-1911115380

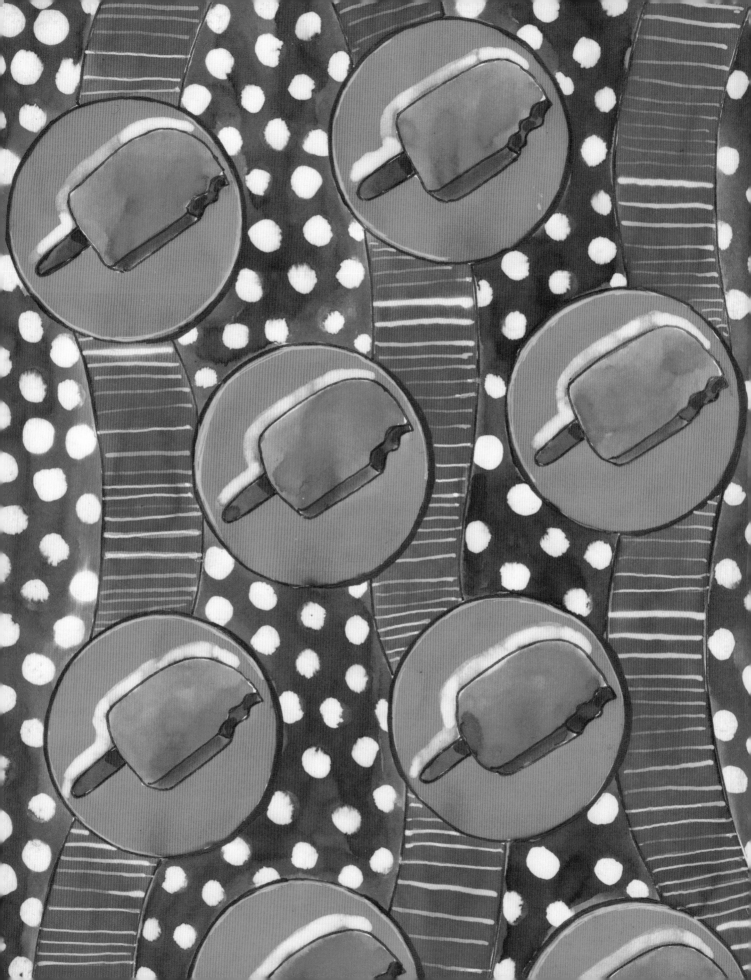